W9-DDQ-224

Max and Zoe

Too Many Tricks

by Shelley Swanson Sateren

illustrated by Mary Sullivan

PICTURE WINDOW BOOKS
a capstone imprint

Max and Zoe is published by Picture Window Books
A Capstone Imprint
1710 Roe Crest Drive
North Mankato, Minnesota 56003
www.capstonepub.com

Library of Congress Cataloging-in-Publication Data
Sateren, Shelley Swanson.
 Max and Zoe : too many tricks / by Shelley Swanson Sateren ;
illustrated by Mary Sullivan.
     p. cm. -- (Max and Zoe)
 Summary: It is April Fool's Day, but Max needs to learn that not all
pranks are funny.
  ISBN 978-1-4048-7197-7 (library binding)
 ISBN 978-1-4795-2327-6 (paperback)
1. April Fools' Day--Juvenile fiction. 2. Practical jokes--Juvenile
fiction. 3. Elementary schools--Juvenile fiction. 4. Best friends--
Juvenile fiction. [1. April Fools' Day--Fiction. 2. Practical jokes--
Fiction. 3. Elementary schools--Fiction. 4. Schools--Fiction. 5. Best
friends--Fiction. 6. Friendship--Fiction.] I. Sullivan, Mary, 1958- ill. II.
Title. III. Title: Too many tricks. IV. Series: Sateren, Shelley Swanson.
Max and Zoe.
 PZ7.S249155Mdx 2013
 813.54--dc23
                                                2012047383

Designer: Kristi Carlson

Printed in China by Nordica.
0314/CA21400182
022014   007226NORDF13

Table of Contents

It was April Fool's Day. Max couldn't wait to trick his best friend, Zoe.

Before school, Max stuffed his backpack with supplies for pranks.

Max got to the bus stop before

Zoe. He told all the other kids to

hide behind the bushes.

When Zoe arrived, he yelled,

"We missed the bus!"

"Oh no!" Zoe said.

"April Fool's!" Max laughed.

So did all of the other kids.

"Very funny!" Zoe said.

"Do you want a piece of gum?" Max asked.

"Sure," Zoe said. "Thanks, Max!"

As Zoe started chewing the gum, the other kids started to point at her.

Her face turned red. "Hey," she said. "What's going on?"

"Your teeth are all black. April Fool's!" Max yelled and laughed. Everyone else did, too. Everyone except Zoe.

At school, Max put something in Zoe's desk.

A minute later, she opened her desk and screamed, "Ahhhh! A spider!"

Their teacher, Ms. Young, hurried over. "It's just a toy," she said. "And who does this belong to?"

"Me! April Fool's!" Max laughed.

The whole class laughed.

Zoe's face turned bright red.
She was so embarrassed. She knew
Max was trying to be funny, but it
wasn't funny to her.

After morning break, the

school's fire bell rang. Ms. Young

looked surprised.

"Everyone line up," she

said. "Hurry, class. Quietly and

quickly!"

A cold wind blew and ice covered the mud puddles. Everyone shivered on the playground.

"What a terrible day for a fire drill," Max thought.

Max tried to stand next to Zoe, but she moved away from him.

"What's your problem?" Max asked.

But Zoe was already too far away to hear him. Without Zoe by his side, Max was bored.

Max started to goof around. He
jumped up and down on a frozen
puddle. CRACK!

Cold water filled Max's shoes.

"Oh no!" Max said.

Just then, Max heard sirens. Fire trucks sped into the parking lot.

"This is the longest fire drill ever," Max muttered.

Twenty minutes later, everyone was allowed back inside.

"Was there a real fire?" Max asked.

"No. Someone pulled the fire bell for a prank," said Ms. Young.

"Well, it wasn't funny!" Max

said, staring at his wet shoes.

"It sure wasn't," Ms. Young said.

"Hmm," Max thought. "Maybe some pranks aren't funny. I better not put green food coloring in Zoe's milk. I won't put honey on her pencil, either."

Before lunch, Max found Zoe.

"I guess not all pranks are funny. I'm sorry," he said.

She smiled. "That's okay. Want to sit together at lunch?"

"Yeah!" said Max.

While they were eating, Zoe
turned away from Max.

She turned back and Max cried,
"Zoe! Your nose is bleeding!"

She laughed. "April Fool's, Max! It's just ketchup!"

Everyone at the table laughed, too.

"Ha!" Max laughed. "That's a good prank, Zoe."

"Thanks," she said. "But don't worry. I won't play more tricks on you today. It's not funny to keep doing pranks to the same person."

"You're right," said Max. "Next year I won't be an April fool. I'll be an April smart!"

Zoe grinned. "Sounds like a plan."

About the Author

Shelley Swanson Sateren is the award-winning author of many children's books. She has worked as a children's book editor and in a children's bookstore. Today, besides writing, Shelley works with elementary-school-aged children in various settings. She lives in St. Paul, Minnesota, with her husband and two sons.

About the Illustrator

Mary Sullivan has been drawing and writing her whole life, which has mostly been spent in Texas. She earned her BFA from the University of Texas in Studio Art, but she considers herself a self-trained illustrator. Mary lives in Cedar Park, a suburb of Austin, Texas.

Glossary

drill **(DRIL)** — to teach someone how to do something by having the person do it over and over again

embarrassed **(em-BARE-whsst)** — felt awkward and uncomfortable

prank **(PRANGK)** — a playful trick

shivered **(SHIV-urd)** — shook from the cold

siren **(SYE-ruhn)** — a machine that makes a loud, high sound

Discussion Questions

1. Have you ever played a prank on someone? Has anyone played a prank on you? What happened?

2. Do you think April Fool's Day is fun or not? Explain your answer.

3. Max made Zoe feel bad. Discuss a time you made a friend feel bad. How did you make him/her feel better?

Writing Prompts

1. It's important to stay safe when playing pranks on people. Make a list of three safe pranks.

2. Do you think Max was being a good friend to Zoe? Write three sentences explaining your answer.

3. Write a paragraph about your favorite prank from the story.

Make an April Fool's Day Card

Max and Zoe play pranks on each other. Make this card and you can fool someone, too!

What you need:

• 1 sheet of white paper

• glue stick

• color pencils or markers

What you do:

1. Fold the sheet of paper in half. With your finger, press the fold line flat.

2. Open the paper back up. Now you have two rectangles, side by side. Cover the right rectangle with glue, except for about half of an inch at the edges.

3. Fold the two halves together again. Press on top so the glue sticks.

4. On top of the card, write HAPPY APRIL FOOL'S DAY! If you like, draw a funny picture, too.

5. Give the card to a friend or someone in your family. Laugh as they try to open the card!

The Fun Doesn't Stop Here!

Discover more at www.capstonekids.com

- Videos & Contests
- Games & Puzzles
- Friends & Favorites
- Authors & Illustrators

Find cool websites and more books like this one at www.facthound.com. Just type in the Book ID 9781404871977 and you're ready to go!

E R/S
Level 1

Sateren, Shelley
    Swanson.

Max and Zoe.

JUN 0 5 2015

DATE			

8/17- 9